Goldilocks
and the Three Bears

Bath · New York · Cologne · Melbourne · Delhi
Hong Kong · Shenzhen · Singapore

Four steps for enjoyable reading

Traditional stories and fairy tales are a great way to begin reading practice. The stories and characters are familiar and lively. Follow the steps below to help your child become a confident and independent reader:

Step 1
Read the story aloud to your child. Run your finger under the words as you read.

One day, Goldilocks was walking in the woods. Yum! She could smell something tasty. It was coming from a little house.

4

Step 2
Look at the pictures and talk about what is happening.

Step 3

Read the simple text on the right-hand page together. When reading, some words come up again and again, such as **the**, **to**, and **and**. Your child will quickly get to recognize these high-frequency words by sight.

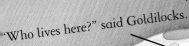

"Who lives here?" said Goldilocks.

Step 4

When your child is ready, encourage them to read the simple lines on their own.

5

One day, Goldilocks was walking in the woods. Yum! She could smell something tasty. It was coming from a little house.

"Who lives here?" said Goldilocks.

Goldilocks knocked on the door.
But there was no reply. Goldilocks
pushed the door. It swung open,
but there was no one there.
Goldilocks stepped inside!

There were three bowls of hot
porridge on the table.

The tasty smell was making Goldilocks feel hungry! She tasted the big bowl of porridge. It was too salty.

Next, she tasted the middle-size bowl of porridge. It was too sweet.

Finally, she tasted the little bowl of porridge. . . .

It was just right! Goldilocks ate
it all up.

Goldilocks needed to sit
down after all that
yummy porridge.
She sat on the
big chair. It
was too high.

She sat on the
middle-size chair.
It was too low.

She sat on the little chair. . . .

Oh no! Goldilocks broke the little chair!

Goldilocks crept upstairs. There were three beds. She tried the big bed. It was too hard.

She tried the middle-size bed. It was too soft.

She tried the little bed. . . .

It was just right! Goldilocks
took a nap.

But while Goldilocks was asleep,
three hungry bears came back
to the house. They were looking
forward to eating their porridge!

The three bears looked at their bowls of porridge.

"Who's been eating my porridge?" roared Daddy Bear. "Who's been eating my porridge?" growled Mommy Bear. "Who's eaten my porridge ALL UP?" squeaked Baby Bear.

"What will I eat?" cried Baby
Bear. He was sad.

"Who's been sitting in my chair?" roared Daddy Bear.

"Who's been sitting in my chair?" growled Mommy Bear.

"Who's been sitting in my chair and has BROKEN IT?" squeaked Baby Bear.

"Where will I sit?" said Baby Bear.

"Who's been sleeping in my bed?" roared Daddy Bear.

"Who's been sleeping in my bed?" growled Mommy Bear.

"Who is IN my bed?" said
Baby Bear.

Suddenly, Goldilocks woke up and saw three bears! She jumped up and ran away. And the three bears never saw her again!

She ran as fast as she could, all
the way home.

23